SPECIAL THANKS TO ANNE MARIE RYAN
FOR GABBY EVANS, JACQUELINE SHAKESPEARE AND
DEBRA BOOKER, MY SUPERMUM FRIENDS

ORCHARD BOOKS
Carmelite House
50 Victoria Embankment
London EC4Y 0DZ

First published by Orchard Books in 2017

THE POWERPUFF GIRLS, CARTOON NETWORK,
the logos, and all related characters and elements are trademarks of
and © Cartoon Network.

A CIP catalogue record for this book is available
from the British Library.

ISBN 978 1 40834 707 2

1 3 5 7 9 10 8 6 4 2

Printed and bound by CPI Group (UK) Ltd, Croydon, CR0 4YY

Orchard Books
An imprint of Hachette Children's Group
Part of The Watts Publishing Group Limited
An Hachette UK Company
www.hachette.co.uk

MIX
Paper from
responsible sources
FSC
www.fsc.org   FSC® C104740

The paper and board used in this book are made from wood from responsible sources.

the POWERPUFF GIRLS™

BRAIN FREEZE

MEET THE POWERPUFF GIRLS!

Favourite colour: Pink
Aura power: Sponge, broom, stapler
Likes: Organising, stationery, science, punching baddies and doing well at school
Dislikes: Mess, being disorganised
Most likely to say: "Let's go save the day!"

BLOSSOM

Favourite colour: Blue
Likes: Animals, creating computer games, make-up, punching baddies, singing, her toy octopus, Octi
Dislikes: Animals being upset, dressing up in ugly clothes
Most likely to say: "I love piggies!"

BUBBLES

Favourite colour: Green
Aura power: Rocket, tank, submarine, cannon
Likes: Roller derby, fighting, deathball
Dislikes: Dressing up, wussy people
Most likely to say: "Don't call me princess!"

BUTTERCUP

THE PROFESSOR: The Powerpuff Girls' father, the Professor, was trying to create the perfect little girls out of sugar and spice and all things nice. But when he accidentally added Chemical X to the mix, he got three super cute and super fierce crime-fighting superheroes: The Powerpuff Girls!
Likes: Science, The Powerpuff Girls, creating new inventions in his lab under the house
Dislikes: When things explode
Most likely to say: "How could you hate science?"

MOJO JOJO:
Evil monkey mastermind Mojo Jojo is always trying to wreak havoc on The Powerpuff Girls.
Likes: Dressing up, trying to take over Townsville
Dislikes: The Powerpuff Girls!
Most likely to say: "Curses!"

THE NARRATOR:

Ahem, and there's me. I'm your friendly narrator. I'll pop up now and again to give you all the gossip on what's going on. Are you sitting comfortably? No? Well then get ready! Honestly, do I have to do everything around here? The book's about to begin! Ready? Then let's go!

CONTENTS

BREAKFAST BITES BACK

It was quiet at Professor Utonium's house in the city of Townsville. Suspiciously quiet …

"What are you girls up to?" said the Professor, popping his head around the living room door.

"Shhh, Professor! We're watching *Kung Fu Super Puppies*," snapped Buttercup.

The Powerpuff Girls were on the sofa, their big, round eyes glued to the screen.

"It's one of our favourite shows," explained Blossom, without turning away from the TV. "If the puppies beat the Karate Cats they'll earn super-powered black collars!"

Three adorable puppies on the TV screen suddenly launched into a rap battle with a big gang of mean-looking cats.

"YEAH, WE'RE THE KUNG FU PUPPIES
AND WE DON'T BACK DOWN,
FIGHTIN' CRIME AND BADDIES
ON THE STREETS OF DOGTOWN.
WE MIGHT BE SMALL, BUT WE'RE REALLY TOUGH,
BIG IT UP FOR THE DOGGIES, RUFF RUFF RUFF!"

"I really don't understand this show," the Professor sighed, shaking his head and leaving the room.

"I LOVE the Kung Fu Super Puppies!" squealed Bubbles. "They're sooooo CUTE!!!"

On the screen, the cats surrounded the puppies with their teeth and claws bared. The cats' leader stepped forward and hissed, "I, Tabi, will stop you pesky puppies from returning to the Doghouse Dojo."

"You'll be coughing up furballs when we're done with you," a bulldog puppy growled defiantly.

"Awesome, dude!" whooped Buttercup.

Snarling, the cats attacked the three puppies in a flurry of fur. Tabi swiped at a basset hound puppy with her claws. He spun round and blocked her with his tail. **POW!**

Then his long ears started to spin and the puppy rose up in the air. Flying above the cats, he aimed kicks at the baddies with his paws.

"Smart move!" said Blossom. Next to her, Buttercup was hovering in the air, copying the puppies' kicks and punches.

"It would be so fun to have helicopter ears like the Kung Fu Puppies," Bubbles said longingly. "Then I could fly!"

"You *can* fly," Blossom said.

"Oh yeah!" giggled Bubbles, turning a loop-the-loop in the air.

On the screen, Tabi charged at a fluffy white poodle, her claws out. The puppy hit back with a paw chop, but the cat caught the pompom at the end of the poodle's tail in her paws.

"Oh no! Poor little puppy!" cried Bubbles as Tabi spun the poodle in the air by the tail.

The bulldog puppy charged to his friend's rescue. He pounced on Tabi, pinning the baddie to the ground under his paws. Then the other two puppies grabbed a box of dog biscuits and started firing them at the cats. As the bone-shaped biscuits whizzed through the air, the cats fled.

"Nice teamwork, guys!" cheered Blossom, hovering off the sofa.

But before they found out whether the puppies had earned their super-powered black collars, an advertisement filled the TV screen.

**IT'S SO CREAMY! IT'S SO DREAMY!
COME QUICK AND GET YOUR KICKS
AT LICKETY SPLITS ICE CREAM PARLOUR!
I SCREAM!
YOU SCREAM!
WE ALL SCREAM FOR—**

"Ice cream!" shrieked Buttercup, Blossom and Bubbles, shattering the round living room windows with their screams.

Buttercup grabbed the remote control and pressed the pause button. "Must. Have. Ice cream!"

"That's funny, I was just thinking the exact same thing!" cried Blossom, flying towards the door. "Let's go!"

"Yippee!" squealed Bubbles. "Creamy dreamy ice cream!!!!"

Despite having superhuman abilities, The Powerpuff Girls were not immune to the power of advertising. Now, if you'll excuse me, I'm suddenly craving chocolate ice cream …

SWOOSH! In a blaze of pink, green and blue light, The Powerpuff Girls zipped to the centre of Townsville and landed outside Lickety Splits Ice Cream Parlour. The shop had a striped awning and a huge plastic ice cream cone outside it. There was a poster hanging in the window.

"Look!" Blossom said, her eyes shining with excitement.

ENTER OUR CREAMY DREAMY CONTEST!
INVENT A NEW FLAVOUR AND
WIN FREE ICE CREAM FOR A YEAR!

"Free ice cream for a year?" said Buttercup. "Outta the way!" She pulled open the door and marched inside.

Blossom and Bubbles followed her. "Mmmmmm!" they all sighed, gazing at the freezer full of ice cream.

"Caramel crunch, raspberry ripple, mint chocolate chip ..." read Blossom.

"They all look sooooo good!" said Bubbles. "How will we choose?"

"Easy," said Buttercup. "We'll have the Superhero Sundae with a scoop of every flavour," she told the man behind the counter. "Oh – and three spoons."

The sundae came in an enormous dish and was smothered in toffee and chocolate sauce and clouds of whipped cream. It was topped with nuts, sprinkles and a red cherry.

"That sure is a big sundae," the man behind the counter said. "Sure you can manage it, princess?"

"I'm NOT a princess!" growled Buttercup, her eyes narrowing dangerously. She picked up the sundae and tossed it down her throat in one gulp.

BUURRRRPPP!

"Hit me again, dude," she said, plonking the empty sundae cup back on the counter.

The ice cream man quickly made another sundae and Buttercup carried it over to the table where her sisters were sitting. They tucked in eagerly.

"Hey! Quit hogging all the whipped cream, Blossom," grumbled Buttercup.

"Dee-licious!" sighed Bubbles happily, taking a bite of rocky road.

"Ahem!" Blossom tapped her spoon against the side of the sundae cup to get her sisters' attention. "If we're going to win this contest we need a plan. What new flavour should we invent?"

"Maybe the Professor could help us," suggested Bubbles.

"Yeah, right," snorted Buttercup, "if we want Chemical X as our secret ingredient."

Flashback! Professor Utonium accidentally added Chemical X to the mix when he created The Powerpuff Girls. Oopsie! It had given them their superhero powers. But it probably wouldn't taste very good in ice cream ...

"I've got an idea," said Blossom. "How about nice and simple strawberry with rainbow sprinkles?"

"BORING!" scoffed Buttercup.

"Strawberry's nice," said Bubbles sweetly. "But I was thinking of something special." She took a deep breath. "How about Scrummy Yummy Tutti Frutti Chewy Gooey Bluey Bubblegum?"

Blossom and Buttercup both shook their heads.

"We need something that's really going to blow people's minds – and their tastebuds," Buttercup said.

"So what did you have in mind?" Blossom asked.

"Pizza," said Buttercup, leaning back in her chair proudly.

"Yuck! Nobody will want to eat pizza-flavoured ice cream," said Blossom.

"Says who?" demanded Buttercup. "Everyone likes pizza!"

"That's true," said Bubbles, nodding. "I like pizza."

"Ice cream is supposed to be sweet," argued Blossom.

"Duh! It's *Hawaiian* pizza," said Buttercup. "With pineapple."

"Let's take a vote," said Blossom. "I say strawberry."

"Bubblegum!" said Bubbles.

"Pizza!" said Buttercup.

Grrr!

The three girls narrowed their eyes. Bright pink light beamed from Blossom's eyes, blue light from Bubbles's eyes, and green light from Buttercup's eyes. The heat from their glares turned their Superhero Sundae into a gooey puddle.

"There's only one possible solution," said Blossom grimly.

"What?" asked Bubbles.

"The Professor can decide," Blossom said. "Whichever flavour he says is best is the one we'll put in the competition – the other two have to back down. Agreed?"

Bubbles nodded. "May the best sister win."

"Every girl for herself," said Blossom.

"Bring. It. ON!" said Buttercup.

MAY THE BEST FLAVOUR WIN!

So The Powerpuff Girls are all going to try and make the best ice cream flavour. I'm sure they won't let a bit of healthy competition come between them ...

"The simplest solution is always the best," said Blossom happily. "That's why my strawberry with rainbow sprinkles is going to be the clear winner."

"Yeah – winner of the 'most boring flavour ever' competition," scoffed Buttercup. "Unlike my awesome pineapple pizza ice cream."

Blossom scowled at her sister.

"There's something for everyone in my Scrummy Yummy Tutti Frutti Chewy Gooey Bluey Bubblegum flavour," Bubbles said sweetly. "That's why it is the best."

"The best way to make someone sick," Blossom muttered.

"Now, now, girls!" said Professor Utonium, holding up his hands. "Stop squabbling! Why don't you tell me what's going on?"

The girls were in the Professor's lab in the basement of their house. It was full of gleaming machines with mysterious buttons.

There was a strange pink potion bubbling away in a glass flask and test tubes filled with a murky green liquid.

"Lickety Splits ice cream parlour is having a contest," explained Blossom. "The new flavour that gets the most votes wins a year's supply of free ice cream."

The three girls all sighed, a dreamy look in their big eyes as they imagined all of that creamy, dreamy ice cream.

"So what flavour do *you* think sounds best, Professor?" Bubbles said, batting her eyelashes.

"Well, a scientist always requires proof before he or she reaches a conclusion," said Professor Utonium.

The girls stared at him blankly.

"Dude, say it in English," said Buttercup.

an experiment,"
fessor with a chuckle.
He added a few drops of the
green liquid to the pink
potion in the flask. It fizzed,
making a cloud of smoke
that smelled like pickled
onions. "You can't decide
which flavour is the
best unless you actually
taste them."

The Powerpuff Girls
exchanged looks. It was the
perfect way to settle their
argument – AND eat more
ice cream.

"Professor, you're a
genius!" said Blossom.

"But we don't know how to make ice cream!" cried Bubbles.

> *If only there was a machine that could help them. Oh, wait ...*

"I've got just the thing!" exclaimed Professor Utonium. "My latest invention is the Utonium Churn-o-Meter. I designed it to measure sickness on roller coasters – the more it shakes, the more fun the roller coaster is. Did you know that motion sickness is caused when the brain gets mixed signals from your eyes and inner ear?"

"Fascinating," said Buttercup, rolling her eyes.

The Professor led them over to a shiny metal machine. There was a massive silver drum and a dial. He pulled a red lever.

With a deep rumble, the machine roared into life. The drum started to turn and the needle on the dial moved to **BUTTERFLIES IN TUMMY**. It started to spin faster and the needle crept up to **QUITE QUEASY**.

Professor Utonium pressed the 'Barf Booster' button and the drum rotated even faster and started to shake up and down. The needle moved to **PUKE ALERT**.

"Cool!" said Buttercup.

The machine was shaking violently now. The needle inched towards **I'M GONNA HURL** and a siren started to wail.

"What does this one do?" Bubbles asked, pressing a button marked **WARP SPEED**.

The machine was moving so fast it looked like a blur. The needle reached **THAR SHE BLOWS!!!** and an alarm blared.

Professor Utonium pulled the lever down and the machine stopped instantly.

"That's very impressive," said Blossom. "But how does it help us?"

Professor Utonium pressed a blue button marked **DEEP FREEZE** and a blast of cold air puffed out of the machine.

"This was meant to cool down the roller coaster riders when they felt too ill," the Professor explained, "but I'm sure it will work for us instead. Just pop your ingredients into the drum and the Churn-o-Meter will do all the hard work."

WHOOSH!

Blossom, Bubbles and Buttercup flew out of the room as fast as they could, leaving a sparkling trail of pink, blue and green light behind them.

Meanwhile, on Monster Island, someone else was concocting a recipe. But it wasn't for ice cream — it was a recipe for DISASTER!

Mojo Jojo, the monkey supervillain, hummed as he arranged a display of travel brochures on a desk made out of cardboard boxes. He quickly stuck posters of beaches and city skyscrapers on the nearby palm trees. Then he pulled on a flowery dress with a nametag that said 'Jojo'.

He rubbed his green hands together as he pulled up a flip pad and reviewed his cunning new plan. "First, Mojo will defeat The Powerpuff Girls! Next, Mojo will take over Townsville! *Mwa ha ha!*" He sat at the desk of the fake travel agency and waited for his first customers to arrive.

A huge monster with three eyes, four arms, a waistcoat and a moustache was smashing up a nearby rock.

"Yoo hoo!" Mojo Jojo called out. "Do you require a holiday?

The monster stopped and thought. "Why, yes!" it boomed in a posh voice. "Yes, I believe I could do with a break."

"It is hard work being a monster," Mojo Jojo said soothingly. "You deserve a holiday and that is why I, Mojo Jojo, have a fantastic offer for you today – free tickets to Townsville!" He showed the monster a brochure. "It is the ideal destination for a monster in need of relaxation."

> *A bit of advice, monsters – if it sounds too good to be true, it probably is.*

The posh monster nodded and Mojo Jojo
handed it a ticket.

A lizard monster with a long orange
tongue stopped to peer at the posters.

"Pardon me," Mojo Jojo said. "You look
like you could use a break."

"I always look like this," grumbled the
lizard monster.

"Then you will love Townsville," said Mojo Jojo, giving the monster a winning smile. "There are many beautiful people there."

Soon, there was a long line of monsters eager to visit Townsville.

"Do not worry, everyone can come," Mojo Jojo reassured them, handing a ticket to a three-eyed worm monster. "It is the hottest ticket in town," he said. Then under his breath he added, "The hottest ONE-WAY ticket in town!"

Mojo Jojo was sending monsters to Townsville – and they weren't coming back!

VOTES FOR ICE CREAM!

And now, for the moment of truth … drum roll please … the ice creams are ready!

"Ta da!" said Professor Utonium. He opened the machine's drum and scooped out lots of pink ice cream with brightly coloured flecks. "This one is Blossom's," he said, handing each Powerpuff Girl a cone.

"Yum!" said Blossom, her face lighting up as she tried her ice cream. "It's just how I wanted it – nice and simple."

"It's quite tasty," said Bubbles politely.

"Not bad," Buttercup admitted, eating her ice cream – cone and all – in one gulp. **BUURRRRPPPP!** "But not that good, either."

"This one's yours, Bubbles," said the Professor. He took a container of bright blue ice cream with swirls out of a freezer and handed round samples. "What do you call it again?"

"Scrummy Yummy Tutti Frutti Chewy Gooey Bluey Bubblegum," Bubbles said, licking her ice cream happily. "It's got everything you could want."

"Sometimes less is more," Blossom said. She tried to spit out a wad of bubblegum, but accidentally spat out a mouthful of blue ice cream instead.

"And last but not least," said Professor Utonium, taking out another container of ice cream, "this is Buttercup's pizza flavour."

"Now you're talking," said Buttercup, grabbing the first cone. "Oh yeah, I'm getting cheese … and a hint of tomato … and nice big chunks of pineapple."

"*I'm* getting sick," said Blossom, throwing her cone in the bin.

"Now that we've tried all of them, we can decide which one is best," said Bubbles. "Mine, right?"

"Mine," said Blossom.

"Mine," said Buttercup.

Grrrrrrrrrrrrr. The girls glared at each other, hands on their hips.

"You decide, Professor," said Blossom.

Professor Utonium looked worried. "Oh, but they all look delicious. I couldn't possibly choose between them …"

"Don't worry. We can take it if we lose," Bubbles said, her bottom lip wobbling.

"Shut your eyes – then it will be fair," said Blossom.

The Professor reluctantly closed his eyes. First, Bubbles fed him a spoonful of her ice cream.

"Lovely," said Professor Utonium.

Next, Blossom gave him a taste of hers.

"Yummy," said the Professors.

Next, Buttercup gave him a sample of her ice cream.

"Er – very interesting," said Professor Utonium, his face turning slightly green.

Suddenly, the Professor clutched his head. His face scrunched up in agony and he howled in pain.

"Buttercup, your gross pizza ice cream is hurting the Professor!" cried Bubbles in alarm.

"No, it's not that," choked out Professor Utonium. "It's – it's— BRAIN FREEZE!"

> The scientific name for brain freeze is sphenopalatine ganglioneuralgia.
> Try saying that three times fast.

"I'm sorry, girls," said the Professor when he had recovered. "I must've eaten the ice cream too fast and it gave me a brain freeze headache. All the flavours are delicious. I really can't decide between them."

He thought for a moment. "Hmmm. I wonder if I could invent some kind of machine that could select the best flavour *scientifically* ..." He hurried over to his work bench and started sketching a design.

The Powerpuff Girls looked at each other and sighed.

"We can't wait for the Professor to design a machine," said Blossom. "We're all going to have to enter the contest separately."

"Don't worry," said Bubbles kindly. "When I win I'll share my year's supply of ice cream with both of you."

"I won't," said Buttercup.

"Buttercup!" Blossom scolded.

SWOOSH!

The Powerpuff Girls took off, each flying in a different direction.

32

"Vote for Strawberry Sprinkles!" Blossom called through a megaphone. She was standing on a crate outside a busy shopping centre. She handed out badges with pictures of pink ice cream cones on them to everyone who went past. Every billboard in Townsville was plastered with a huge picture of Blossom reading: "Keep it Simple. Vote for Strawberry Sprinkles."

"Strawberry Sprinkles sounds wonderful," said an old lady. "I hope you win."

"Thank you for your support!" Blossom said politely.

Next, Blossom pinned one of her badges on to a little boy's T-shirt.

"Do you have any samples?" he asked.

33

"The girl with the big blue eyes gave me some of her ice cream."

"What?" said Blossom, nearly falling off her crate.

The boy pointed down the street, where Bubbles was pedalling an ice cream cart down the road. Along the way, she was stopping and handing out free samples of her bubblegum ice cream to everyone she passed. She stopped at a family with a little girl and a teenage boy.

"Try the best new ice cream flavour in town," she called. "Vote for Scrummy Yummy Tutti Frutti Chewy Gooey Bluey Bubblegum!" She handed one to the girl. "My ice cream will blow your mind – and bubbles too!"

"Yum!" said the little girl as she tasted it.

"It's fruity AND chewy."

"What more could you want?" said Bubbles. She smiled at the little girl. "You're soooooooooo cute!"

"You've got my vote, Bubbles," said the girl's mum.

Blossom glared at Bubbles. "Ask not what you can do for your ice cream," she shouted through her megaphone, "but what your ice cream can do for you! EVERYONE! Repeat after me. Vote Strawberry Sprinkles! Vote Strawberry Sprinkles ..."

But her chant was drowned out by a loud **ZOOOOOOOOOOOOOM!**

Everyone looked up and saw a streak of green light in the sky. Buttercup was flying overhead with a banner trailing behind her that read, **"DON'T BE A WIMP. VOTE PIZZA!"**

"Ooooohhhhh!" gasped the crowd as Buttercup did daring dives and turned impressive loop-the-loops in the air.

"Cool!" said the little girl's teenaged brother. "Pizza ice cream sounds wicked."

"It sounds disgusting," said his father, who was wearing a Strawberry Sprinkles badge.

"Well, I like the bubblegum flavour," said the girl, blowing a bubble.

"Me too," said her mother.

"No way," said the teenage boy. "Pizza is the best!" He jabbed a finger at the girl's bubble. **POP!** The bubble burst.

"Hey!" she cried, peeling gum off her face. "Hands off my bubblegum!"

Soon, a group of bubblegum supporters started chanting: **"BUBBLE-GUM! BUBBLE-GUM!"**

"Let's hear it for Strawberry Sprinkles," Blossom yelled into her megaphone.

Everyone wearing a strawberry badge let out a loud cheer.

Suddenly, Buttercup swooped down, scattering the strawberry and bubblegum supporters. "Make some noise if you want pizza ice cream," she called.

The teenage boy and the other pizza fans whooped at the top of their lungs.

Blossom, Bubbles and Buttercup glared at each other. The groups of strawberry, bubblegum and pizza supporters glared at each other.

TROUBLE IN TOWNSVILLE

On Monster Island, the monsters were getting ready for their holiday in Townsville. Hey, monsters — don't forget to pack sunscreen!

"Attention, please! Monster Jet Flight 666 to Townsville will be departing in ten minutes' time," Mojo Jojo announced into a microphone.

The evil monkey had changed into a flight attendant's uniform with tights, a jaunty blue hat and a scarf around his neck. "All monsters holding tickets, please proceed to the departure gate."

There was a stampede as monsters charged towards a boarding area made up of folding chairs, shoving each other with clawed hands and whacking each other with their spiked tails.

"Tree Crab Monster?" Mojo Jojo called out from his checklist. A monster with tusks, long vines and legs like a crab shuffled forward. "Three-eyed Worm Monster?" A huge worm slithered forward.

"Lizard Monster? Volcano Monster … step forward, come along now. Mojo does not have all day."

"I hear that Townsville has several excellent theatres," said the posh monster. It turned to the other monsters excitedly. "I've always wanted to see an opera," it said, waving a pair of glasses with three lenses.

"Townsville has wonderful museums, too," said the lizard monster, waving its claws. "I just can't wait to destroy them."

"RAAAAAAARH!" agreed the volcano monster, ignoring the 'No Smoking' sign and letting out a blast of flames from its head.

"Don't worry," Mojo Jojo assured the monsters. "There are plenty of buildings to destroy in Townsville. Mojo is sure you'll love it so much there you'll want to stay." Under his breath, he added, "*For ever!*"

The tree crab monster pointed at the horned monster's passport and gave a deep mocking laugh. **"HUHHH HUHH HUHH."**

"MWRR?" The horned monster glared at the tree crab monster. The tree crab monster pointed and nudged the volcano monster, who looked at the photo and started sniggering.

"YRRRRGH!" the horned monster bellowed, launching itself at the other two.

"Save it for when we arrive," said Mojo Jojo, breaking up the fight. Under his breath he muttered, "Those Powerpuff Girls won't know what's hit them."

"Oh no! I forgot my passport!" cried the lizard monster in a panic.

"Do not worry!" said Mojo Jojo, shoving the monster on to the plane. "Mojo will make an exception just this once. Don't forget to send a postcard!"

Finally, Mojo Jojo had loaded all of the monsters on to the plane. He slammed the door behind him and swapped his flight attendant's hat for a pilot's hat.

"At last!" he chortled, stepping into the cockpit. "Next stop – annihilation of The Powerpuff Girls!" He drove the plane down the runway and it soared into the air. **ZOOOOOOM!**

"This is Captain Mojo speaking," Mojo Jojo announced. "Sit back, relax and enjoy your flight to Townsville." Then he put the plane on autopilot.

Swapping hats again and stepping out of the cockpit, Mojo Jojo pushed a trolley down the aisle, taking care not to slip on

the lava oozing from the volcano monster. "Enjoy your snack," he called out, flinging bags of pretzels and peanuts at the monsters. "But don't spoil your appetite – there are many delicious things to eat in Townsville. And you can start with three tasty little girls whose names begin with B! *Mwa ha ha!*"

While the monsters were munching their peanuts, the people of Townsville were eating ice cream. Lots and lots of ice cream!

"Blossom's ice cream delivery service – how may I help you?" Blossom said, picking up the telephone. She was sitting in front of a computer, with a complicated schedule open on the screen. Folders full of forms, all carefully filed in alphabetical order, were piled high on her desk.

"If you'd like to place an order for Strawberry Sprinkles you'll need to fill in a few forms," she told the person on the phone as she typed. "I'll also need a recent photograph, a copy of your birth certificate and proof of your address." She peered at the calendar on her screen. "So, you'll get your ice cream in about six weeks. How does that sound? Hello?"

Sighing, Blossom put down the receiver. "How odd," she said to herself. "I think they accidentally hung up on me." She went into the Professor's lab. It had been turned into an ice cream factory. There were now three Churn-o-Meters, each making a different flavour of ice cream round the clock. Blossom went over to the Strawberry Sprinkles machine. She pulled out a tablet and tapped some buttons. A drone flew over, picked up tubs of ice cream and went off to deliver them.

"Oh yes, my system is perfect!" she said, sighing happily.

CRASH! Bubbles flew into the lab and knocked Blossom on to her bottom.

"Oops! Sorry!" Bubbles said, helping her sister back to her feet. "I'm just so busy with my ice cream deliveries. The people of Townsville can't get enough of my Scrummy Yummy Tutti Frutti Chewy Gooey Bluey Bubblegum flavour."

Bubbles grabbed as much bubblegum ice cream as she could hold. "Gotta go!" she cried, flying away in a blaze of blue light.

Sitting nearby playing a computer game, Buttercup laughed.

"What's so funny, lazybones?" asked Blossom as she checked her delivery schedule.

"I've got a MUCH better way to deliver my ice cream," said Buttercup. "Watch!"

She narrowed her eyes and bright green light streamed out of them. The aura quivered in the air then took the shape of a cannon.

"Who wants ice cream?" yelled Buttercup. She loaded her pizza-flavoured ice cream into the cannon and fired it.

BOOM!

Buttercup's ice cream shot out of the cannon and rained down on Townsville. Blossom's drones zoomed overhead and dropped down orders of Strawberry Sprinkles. Meanwhile, Bubbles zipped

around delivering her bubblegum ice cream all over the city.

> We interrupt this story with a severe weather warning for Townsville — take cover, there's an ice cream storm coming!

THUMP! Buttercup's ice cream cannonball hit one of Blossom's drones. **WHUMP!** Ice cream plummeted down, covering the shopping mall. **CRASH!** The damaged drone veered wildly off course and smashed right into Bubbles. **PLOP!** She dropped a month's supply of bubblegum ice cream all over the park.

Bubbles flew back to get more ice cream. She was carrying so much that she couldn't see where she was going. **SMASH!** She collided with another one of Buttercup's pizza-flavoured cannonballs and it crashed into the front of a school, covering it with sticky tomato and pineapple chunks. As Bubbles careened through the air, she bumped into another drone. The drone lost control and crashed into another cannonball, which

exploded all over the town centre. **BOOM!**
An ice cream blizzard snowed down on
Townsville. The city was covered in
ice cream!

Meanwhile, on the Monster Jet flight, Mojo
Jojo was getting ready to land the plane.

"Fasten your seat belts," he announced.
"We are about to begin our descent."

SPLAT!

Strawberry ice cream splattered on the
plane's windscreen.

SPLAT!

Blobs of bubblegum ice cream hit the
plane's wings.

SPLAT!

Pizza-flavoured ice cream pelted the
windows.

"Curses!" shrieked Mojo Jojo.

"EEEEEEEEEKKKKKKKK!" screamed the lizard monster. "We're going to crash!"

A MONSTER MESS

Mmmm … ICE CREAM. It's one of the best things about going on holiday. But not when it's pounding your aeroplane … The monsters' dream holiday was turning into a nightmare!

The tree crab monster wrapped its long vines around the plane, holding it together as Mojo Jojo made an emergency landing.

The plane swerved down the runway, skidding on puddles of melting ice cream. The monsters clambered out of the jet, jostling each other to get their first glimpse of Townsville.

"Hey!" roared the lizard monster, pointing one of its claws. "What's that stuff all over the buildings? It looks such a mess!"

The posh monster squinted at the opera house through its opera glasses and then growled angrily. "This looks nothing like the pictures," he said, putting all four of his hands on his hips.

The worm monster flicked through the pages of its guide-book and hissed in anger.

Furious, the volcano monster spewed out flames and the puddles of pizza-flavoured ice cream around it dried up, leaving only

charred chunks of pineapple behind.

"I demand a refund!" the posh monster said. "Give us one now – or else!"

The other monsters all stepped behind him, growling, hissing and roaring.

"Silence, monsters!" shouted Mojo Jojo. He wanted the monsters to be angry – but not at him! "You dare to threaten Mojo Jojo? I tell you monsters this: you must not seek a refund. You must seek **REVENGE!**"

The monsters advanced on Mojo Jojo, their claws out and their teeth bared.

"No! No! No!" cried Mojo Jojo, jumping up and down. "Not revenge on Mojo! Revenge on those who are responsible for this terrible situation," he said, an evil glint in his eyes. **"THE POWERPUFF GIRLS!"**

> *Did someone mention The Powerpuff Girls? Let's find out what those superhero sisters are up to now.*

Blossom and Buttercup had flown to the centre of Townsville to check out the damage. They waded knee-deep through the

puddles of melted ice
cream that were flooding
the city's streets.

"This is all your fault,
Buttercup!" Blossom
shouted. "This wouldn't
have happened if you had
delivered your ice cream in a properly
organised way."

"MY fault?" shrieked Buttercup. She
pointed at Bubbles. "How is it my fault? SHE
flew right into my cannon fire."

"Me?" squeaked Bubbles, who had
crash-landed in a huge heap of her blue
bubblegum ice cream. "It wasn't ME!
One of HER stupid drones crashed right
into me." She pointed a sticky finger at
Blossom.

The Powerpuff Girls were too busy arguing with each other to notice they had company. And not the sort of company you'd want to turn up unexpectedly.

> *Actually, I never like it when visitors turn up unexpectedly because I like to sit around in my underpants.*

ROAR!

Blossom, Bubbles and Buttercup spun around and their eyes got even bigger than usual. The posh monster had pulled the roof off the opera house and was peering inside it. The tree crab monster was yanking up benches in the park. The three-eyed worm monster was slithering down the high street. And the volcano monster had set fire to a whole row of buildings.

"You Powerpuff Girls have spoiled our holiday!" shouted the lizard monster. "And now you're going to pay for it! **RAAAAAARRRRRRGGHHH!**"

The monsters attacked from every direction. Growling and snarling, they swiped at the girls with their claws, whipped them with spiky tails and snapped at them with sharp teeth.

"I'll handle this!" said Blossom.

"No, I'M the best girl for the job!" said Bubbles.

"Leave it to me!" cried Buttercup.

The Powerpuff Girls STILL can't agree on anything! I have a bad feeling in my stomach about this. But that might be because of the bowl of pizza-flavoured ice cream I just ate ...

Bubbles flew over to the three-eyed worm monster and hit it on the head. **BOP!**

"Poor wormy, you don't want to be scary!" she said.

"Oh, really?" Mojo Jojo shouted. "Show her what you can do!"

The three-eyed worm monster hissed menacingly, rising to its full height. Ready to attack, it towered over the tallest skyscrapers in Townsville.

"Still feeling brave, little girl?" Mojo taunted as the worm monster flicked its forked tongue threateningly.

"WHO ARE YOU CALLING LITTLE?" Bubbles demanded. The worm monster shrank back as a blaze of blue energy shone out of Bubbles and took the shape of a blue giraffe. Bubbles's giraffe kicked at the monster with its long legs but the three-eyed worm monster darted out of reach every time.

Over at the opera house, Buttercup took on the posh monster. She ducked and dived but at least one of its three eyes always spotted her. Buttercup leapt up to aim a punch at the monster, but slipped on a puddle of ice cream.

POW! The punch missed the monster's nose, but shattered its glasses.

"MY OPERA GLASSES! Now how will I see anything on stage?" screeched the posh monster. "This is the worst holiday EVER!"

It snatched Buttercup up in one of its four arms and flung her away through the air.

Buttercup face-planted in a pile of Strawberry Sprinkles.

"Mmmmm, actually this tastes quite good," Buttercup muttered to herself, licking some of Blossom's ice cream off her lips. "Take this, you big bully," she taunted the monster. She hurled an ice cream snowball. **SMACK!** It hit the posh monster right on the end of its nose.

"Well, I never! She hit me!" the monster roared. The enraged monster went on a rampage like the world's biggest toddler having a tantrum. It stomped through the streets of Townsville, crushing cars under its huge scaly feet and ripping up streetlights as it went.

In the park, Blossom was trying to defeat the tree crab monster. It wasn't going well. The monster's thick, bark-covered skin protected it from her punches. Blossom flew at the monster at full speed, but its branches easily batted her aside.

Blossom backed up and tried again, flying at the monster as fast as she could. But this time one of the tree crab monster's vines whipped out and wrapped around her tightly.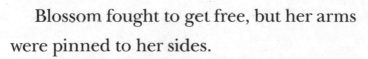

Blossom fought to get free, but her arms were pinned to her sides.

As the tree crab monster waved her in the air, Blossom saw what was going on all around Townsville. The posh monster had Buttercup in a headlock. Bubbles's blue giraffe was losing to the three-eyed worm monster. All across the city, monsters were on the loose, rampaging through streets clogged with ice cream.

Blossom gasped as she realised what was happening. The Powerpuff Girls were ... LOSING!

TIME
OUT

"TIME OUT!" yelled Blossom at the top of her voice. **"TIME. OUT!!!!"**

Everyone froze, even the monsters. The fighting stopped as suddenly as it had begun. The tree crab monster loosened its vines and Blossom fell to the ground.

"Ouch!" she cried.

If you ever have to battle a city full of monsters, the time-out rule is a useful one to remember!

"Huddle up, monsters," called Mojo Jojo. He was wearing a red satin jacket with the words *Mojo's Gym* emblazoned on the back in black lettering. The monsters gathered round him, jogging in place and punching the air like boxers.

Mojo Jojo handed an orange slice to the three-eyed worm monster. It speared it with its fangs and sucked out the juice. "Good job," coached Mojo Jojo. "Keep it up and soon Townsville will be Mojo's." Mojo Jojo corrected himself, "Er, Mojo means OURS."

The other monsters crowded around greedily, shoving as many orange slices as they could into their mouths.

Mojo Jojo gave the tree crab monster a water bottle. "It's important to stay hydrated when you're battling against superheroes," he told it.

The tree crab monster took a long swig of water. Its shrivelled-up leaves turned glossy once more. "Ahhhh!" it sighed.

Mojo Jojo handed the posh monster
a towel. "The Powerpuff Girls are losing.
Keep all three of your eyes on the prize."

The monster mopped its brow. The towel
looked like a face flannel in the enormous
monster's hands. "That little girl broke my
opera glasses ... so I'm going to get her!" it
growled.

"Yes! Do it, do it!" said Mojo Jojo,
clapping the monster on the back.

Over in The Powerpuff Girls' corner,
Blossom huddled together with her sisters.
"The monsters are winning. We need to
change our game plan," she told them.

"It's not my fault!" said Buttercup. "I took
on the biggest monster. What's your excuse?"

"My monster is long AND bitey," said
Bubbles, folding her arms sulkily. "So there."

"Stop!" Blossom cried.
"We should be fighting the
monsters, not each other!
If we don't start pulling
together, we're going
to lose."

"She's right," said Bubbles,
nodding. "We can't win on our own."

"What got us into this situation?" asked
Blossom.

"Duh! A plane-load of monsters," said
Buttercup.

Blossom shook her head. "No. We weren't
getting along *before* they turned up."

Bubbles waved her hand in the air and
jumped up and down excitedly. "Oooooh.
I know! I know!" she cried. "It was the
ICE CREAM!"

"Exactly," said Blossom, nodding. "The ice cream contest caused our problems. But maybe it can solve them too …

Ooooh. Intriguing. What could Blossom mean? I know, but I'm not telling. You'll just have to keep reading to find out.

PHREEEEEEWWWWTTTTT!

Mojo Jojo blew his whistle and the time out was over.

"Awwww! I want more oranges," said the lizard monster.

"You've had enough. Now, get out there and destroy The Powerpuff Girls," said Mojo Jojo, shoving the sticky monster back into battle. "Everyone, take your places. Now, where were we …"

It took a while for everyone to get back into position.

"I think we were like this," said the posh monster, picking Buttercup up in one of its huge hands.

"Actually, I think it was your other hand," Buttercup said. "This arm was smashing that building over there."

"You're quite right," said the posh monster politely, dropping her down and grabbing her with its third arm. "There. That's better."

The tree crab monster wrapped its vines tightly around Blossom and the worm monster rose above Bubbles, poised and ready to strike. When everyone was ready, Mojo Jojo blew his whistle again and the fighting began.

The worm monster hissed, and green venom dripped from its fangs. The giraffe aura headbutted it, then Bubbles zoomed behind the monster and grabbed its tail, then spun it round in circles. Bubbles let it go and it catapulted into the lizard monster, tripping over its tentacles. "Do you mind?" the lizard monster scowled.

"Way to go, Bubbles!" Blossom cheered. Bubbles flew over to give her a high five. As the distracted tree crab monster tried to grab her sister, Blossom wriggled free of the vine. "Now let's go help Buttercup!" she shouted.

Bubbles and Blossom flew over to Buttercup. She'd escaped from the posh monster and was pummelling it.

"Go Buttercup!" cried Blossom and Bubbles. They joined in with the attack, wrapping the posh monster up in its own

arms and tying them together.

"Get them!" bellowed Mojo Jojo from the sidelines.

"I'm a little bit tied up at the moment!" the posh monster called back, struggling to untangle its arms.

"We need to find some ice cream!" shouted Blossom.

The Powerpuff Girls were working together at last. But so were the monsters!

Led by the volcano monster, who had flames bellowing out of its head, a group of angry monsters charged towards them. The monsters stomped down the street, splashing in big puddles of melted ice cream.

"Uh oh," said Bubbles.

"Don't worry. I know how to fight fire," said Blossom. "With ICE!"

She blew out a blast of ice breath. A gust of arctic blue air hit the ice cream puddles, freezing them. Now, the street was as slippery as an ice-skating rink.

"WHOA!" cried the volcano monster as its feet shot out from under itself and it skidded across the icy floor. **CRASH!**

The volcano monster slammed into a department store and reappeared, seconds later, covered in all kinds of hats, dresses and underpants.

"WHEE!" squealed the lizard monster as it slid down the icy street.

"Stop skating and start fighting!" Mojo Jojo screamed at the monsters. Mojo jumped up and down and waved his arms around, but the monsters ignored him. The three-eyed worm monster slid down a mound of bubblegum ice cream.

"I say, this is so much fun!" the posh monster cried.

"Yay!" cried Bubbles, doing a spin. "I want to skate too!"

Don't get distracted, girls. You haven't won yet!

"Um, guys, turn around," said Blossom, with a gulp.

The posh monster, the tree crab monster and the three-eyed worm monster had stopped playing and were heading towards The Powerpuff Girls. The girls tried to escape, but a huge mound of pizza-flavoured ice cream was blocking their way.

"Oh no, we're trapped," wailed Bubbles. "I never thought I wouldn't want to see a big pile of ice cream!"

"It's not ice cream," cried Blossom. "It's AMMUNITION!" She turned to Buttercup. "Quick! We need your cannon!"

Green light poured out of Buttercup as she activated her aura power. In an instant, a glowing cannon was hovering in the air.

Blossom and Bubbles quickly loaded ice cream into it.

BOOM! Ice cream blasted at the monsters. They roared as it pelted them but the monsters didn't stop!

"More ammunition!" screamed Buttercup. Blossom tossed her an ice cream cannonball.

The monsters were close enough to grab the girls now. The lizard monster's tentacles reached out—

Buttercup fired the cannon again and ice cream flew right into the lizard monster's open mouth.

It stopped in its tracks. **"AAARRRGGGGHHHH!"** it howled, clutching its tentacles to its head. **"BRAIN FREEZE!"**

EASY FREEZY

Ouch! I almost feel sorry for the poor monster. Have you ever had brain freeze? It REALLY hurts!

"Yay!" cried Blossom. "The plan's working!"

"I need more ice cream!" shouted Buttercup. "Get me any flavour you can!"

"Aye, aye, captain," said Blossom.

Pink light shot out
of Blossom's eyes as her
laser vision scanned
the area.

"There's lots of
bubblegum ice cream by the
swimming pool," she told Bubbles.

"I'm on it!" Bubbles said, saluting. She
leapt into the air and flew over to the
Townsville pool. Mounds of blue bubblegum
ice cream floated in the water like icebergs.
Using her superhuman strength, Bubbles
lifted all of the ice cream out of the pool and
flew it over to Buttercup.

"Phew!" she said, dropping the blue ice
cream on top of the pizza-flavoured pile.

Blossom's laser vision spotted a supply of
Strawberry Sprinkles by the town hall.

Pink light glowed out of her and took the shape of a vacuum cleaner. Blossom's aura scooped up the strawberry ice cream and dumped it by the cannon.

"Bullseye!" whooped Buttercup as a cannonball of ice cream hit the volcano monster right in the mouth, putting out its flames.

"GRAAAAAAAAH!" the volcano monster shrieked, shivering.

Blossom and Bubbles made cannonballs at the speed of light. Soon all three flavours of ice cream were mixed up together.

Buttercup fired ice cream at the monsters, aiming for their mouths.

"Ha ha!" she laughed. "Those pineapple chunks have gotta hurt!"

The worm monster rose to its full height

and roared, its mouth open wide.

"Ready, aim …" shouted Bubbles, tossing Buttercup a cannonball.

BOOM!

The cannon fired ice cream right into the monster's open mouth.

"HIIIIIIISSSSSSSSSS!" cried the worm monster. As a big bulge of ice cream travelled down its long body, the monster slithered away, moaning in pain.

Buttercup kept up the attack. One after another, the monsters fell to their knees, defeated by brain freeze. Finally, only the posh monster was left standing.

"Your frozen treats won't work against me!" roared the posh monster, its three eyes darting around wildly. "I love eating ice cream in the interval when I go to the theatre."

"Good," retorted Buttercup. "Here's a double helping!"

BOOM! BOOM!

Two ice cream cannonballs landed in the monster's gnashing jaws.

GULP! The monster swallowed it all down in one go.

"Interesting flavour," the monster said. "Got any more?"

Bubbles picked up another ice cream cannonball and Blossom breathed on it with her ice breath, making it as hard as rock. Buttercup loaded the ball into her cannon and aimed it at the monster.

CLONK! The frozen ice cream hit the monster right on the head.

"OWWWW!" the monster screamed, clutching its arms to its head. All three of its eyes fluttered shut and it fell to the ground, flattening a truck underneath it.

"He's out cold," said Bubbles. "Literally."

"I knew ice cream was the solution!" said Blossom happily.

"Get up!" Mojo Jojo shrieked at the monsters. "Are you going to let The Powerpuff Girls ruin your holiday?"

But the monsters ignored him. Their brain freeze had passed and now they were greedily gobbling up all of the ice cream they could get their claws and tentacles on.

"*Nom nom nom nom!* I've never tasted anything like it before. What do you call it?" asked the lizard monster. Its tentacles crammed ice cream into its mouth.

The Powerpuff Girls looked at each other blankly.

"Um ..." Blossom said.

Monster Mish Mash? Pizza with Everything? Townsville Tutti Frutti?

"I know what we can call it," said Bubbles, taking a deep breath. "It's called Scrummy

Yummy Strawberry Sprinkles Tutti Frutti Chewy Gooey Bubblegum Pineapple Pizza!"

"Yeah, that really trips off the tongue," said Buttercup, rolling her eyes.

"How about we call it Powerpuff Girls Surprise?" suggested Blossom.

"That's a great idea!" squealed Bubbles. Buttercup nodded in agreement.

Mojo Jojo knew he was defeated. He quickly changed into an old-fashioned pilot's outfit with a leather jacket, flying helmet and goggles. "Mojo is leaving. The Monster Jet will be making an unscheduled flight back to Monster Island," he called to the monsters. "If you're coming, get on the plane NOW!"

The monsters stomped and slithered to the plane. The posh monster groaned dizzily as the worm monster helped it up.

"This was a terrible holiday," it said, ripping up a stop sign to take home as a souvenir.

"Yes, but the food in Townsville is truly excellent," said the lizard monster, as it stuffed more ice cream in its mouth.

"Next year I'm going to Hawaii," grumbled the posh monster.

Mojo Jojo finally herded all of the monsters back on to the plane. Before slamming the door behind him, he shook his green fist and shouted,
"You accursed
Powerpuff Girls
haven't seen the
last of Mojo!
Mojo will rule
this puny city
one day!"

"I'm sooooo scared," Buttercup jeered.

The Monster Jet soared up into the sky.

"Don't come back soon!" Bubbles sang out sweetly, waving goodbye as the plane disappeared from view.

The Powerpuff Girls high fived.

"Man, I'm starving," said Buttercup. "Is there anything to eat?"

"Er, I hate to point out the obvious," said Blossom, "but how about some ice cream?"

The Powerpuff Girls looked around. Even though the monsters had eaten a lot of the ice cream, there were still huge heaps of Powerpuff Girls Surprise all over Townsville.

Buttercup tossed one of the mixed-up ice cream cannonballs into her mouth. Her green eyes lit up. "It's awesome!" she said. "You guys should try it."

Bubbles licked the ice cream. "Yummy!" she squealed. "I thought my flavour had everything you could want, but it was missing something. It needed strawberries, sprinkles and pineapple pizza!"

Cautiously, Blossom tried a bite of the ice cream. Then she took another bite.

"What do you think?" Bubbles asked her.

Blossom's face broke into a wide grin. "It's the best thing I've ever tasted!"

"Good!" said Buttercup, laughing. "Because we've got a lot of ice cream to clean up!"

ICE CREAM DEEP CLEAN

Townsville was as messy as my face after I've eaten a hot fudge sundae. Luckily, The Powerpuff Girls have an appetite for saving the day.

Blossom, Bubbles and Buttercup had saved the day, but Townsville was a real mess. They looked around at the town in dismay.

All over the city buildings were knocked over and cars were squashed flat. Plus, there was still ice cream everywhere!

"Ready … steady … EAT!" said Buttercup. She flew to the shopping centre and gobbled up all the ice cream she could find.

"Thanks!" cried a shopkeeper. "You Powerpuff Girls are the best."

"It's hard work – but someone's got to do it," Buttercup said, wiping her mouth and giving a burp. Then she used her superhuman strength to pick up all the buildings that the monsters had knocked down.

"Uh!" she grunted, lifting a clothes shop back into place. "Gross!" she said, gagging at the sight of frilly pink dresses in the window display.

Bubbles zipped over to a school that the volcano monster had set alight. If she didn't act fast, it was going to burn down!

"This isn't good," she said. Blue light shone out of her and took the shape of a dolphin. The dolphin aura spat a blast of water out of its mouth and put out the blaze. Then it nudged the slide, the swings and the roundabout back into place with its flippers.

"Thanks, dolphin," said Bubbles.

But there were still piles of ice cream all over the playground.

"I can't eat all of this myself," Bubbles said. Then she had an idea. She started to sing a song. "La la la, la la la!" she trilled, sounding just like the tune of an ice-cream van.

Children came running, drawn by the

sound of Bubbles's music.

"Do you want some ice cream?" Bubbles asked them.

"Yay!" they cheered. The kids quickly ate up all the ice cream.

Meanwhile, Blossom was busy cleaning up a neighbourhood the monsters had wrecked.

"Let's get this tidied up!" Blossom said, rubbing her hands together with excitement. Pink light shone out of her and the next second a vacuum cleaner quivered in the air. Blossom's vacuum cleaner aura sucked up all the nearby rubble and ice cream.

Their work done, The Powerpuff Girls met up back outside Lickety Splits Ice Cream Parlour. It was a mess, too. One of the monsters had ripped off the striped awning and knocked down the big plastic ice cream.

Bubbles and Blossom quickly hung the awning back up, while Buttercup picked up the huge ice cream cone and put it back in place.

The poster announcing the ice cream flavour competition was also lying on the ground. But instead of hanging it back up, Buttercup crumpled the poster up and threw it in the bin. "Slam dunk!" she cried.

The manager ran out of the ice cream shop. "Congratulations, girls!" he told them. "Powerpuff Girls Surprise is the most delicious ice cream flavour I've ever tasted in all my years selling ice cream! You three have won the competition!" He handed them each a large gift certificate. "You've all won a whole year's supply of ice cream. Would you like one now?"

The Powerpuff Girls looked at each other and groaned.

"Ummm, no thanks," said Blossom, shaking her head.

"I'm stuffed!" said Buttercup, clutching her tummy.

"I never want to see ice cream again!" said Bubbles, looking queasy.

"Let's go home," said Blossom.

"That's the best idea you've had all day, Bloss," said Buttercup.

As The Powerpuff Girls flew over Townsville, Blossom looked at her sisters and said, "I'm sorry that I got so carried away with the competition."

"No silly contest is more important than my sisters," agreed Bubbles. "When we stick together, nothing can stop us!"

"Yeah! We kicked those monsters' butts!" said Buttercup.

When they arrived home, Professor Utonium came out of his lab.

"Hello, girls," he said. "Have you been up to anything interesting?"

"Not really," said Buttercup, flopping on the sofa.

"Well, I've been really busy," the Professor told them. "I invented a machine called the Flav-o-matic that scientifically proves the tastiest flavour. You'll never guess what I discovered—"

The Powerful Girls smiled at each other.

"Strawberry, bubblegum and pizza mixed together is the most delicious flavour combination of all," said the Professor.

"Dude, we know," said Buttercup.

The girls snuggled together on the sofa and pressed play on the remote control. The Kung Fu Puppies were at the Doghouse Dojo. Their grand master, an ancient basset hound, put a black collar around each of the puppies' necks.

"By working as a team, you defeated Tabi and her evil kittens," said the grand master in a quavery voice. "That is the way of a true Kung Fu Puppy."

"Yay!" cheered Blossom.

Buttercup did a karate chop in the air. "Woo hoo!" she cried in celebration.

Happy tears rolled down Bubbles's cheeks.

On the television screen, the puppies started rapping.

"WE'RE THE KUNG FU PUPPIES AND OUR PAWS GO POW! WE GOT BLACK COLLARS - BOW WOW WOW WOW!"

"You know, I could use a snack," said Buttercup, switching off the television.

"As long as it's not ice cream," said Blossom.

"How about popcorn?" suggested Bubbles.

"Mmmm … popcorn!" sighed Blossom. "I love salty popcorn with lots of butter."

"No," said Bubbles. "Swect caramel popcorn is the best."

"Are you kidding?" said Buttercup. "Red hot chilli-flavoured popcorn is the only way to go."

"Salty!" shouted Blossom.

"Sweet!" yelled Bubbles.

"Hot!" hollered Buttercup.

Oh no. Here we go again …

THE END

LOVE THIS POWERPUFF GIRLS ADVENTURE?

Then you'll love the next one EVEN MORE! In *Home Super Home*, Blossom, Bubbles and Buttercup face a fiendish plot from stylish supervillains, The Fashionistas!

TURN OVER FOR A SNEAK PEEK!

THE TOASTER
MONSTER

Everyone knows that breakfast is the most important meal of the day. But not many know that toast can be very dangerous. Consider yourself warned!

The Powerpuff Girls were battling an enormous Toaster Monster. Its black cord flicked from side to side like a tail.

Its red lights glowed like evil eyes and its bread slots snapped hungrily at the three superhero sisters.

"Time to pull the plug on this dude," yelled Buttercup. She flew at the monster, pummelling its shiny silver sides with her fists. **BISH! BASH!** But her punches didn't even dent the metal.

The toaster monster rampaged through the streets of Townsville. Shoppers dropped their bags and ran for cover, screaming in fright. The Toaster Monster marched towards an old lady walking her poodle.

"STEP AWAY FROM THAT DOGGIE!" shrieked Bubbles. She streaked through the air, leaving a trail of bright blue light behind her.

Using her superhuman strength, she scooped up the poodle in one arm and its elderly owner in the other. She set them down safely in a park, patted the poodle on the head, then flew back to her sisters.

Bubbles kicked the monster, while Blossom and Buttercup punched and pelted it.

"You're not the only ones who can turn up the heat!" growled the Toaster Monster. Soon, the mouth-watering smell of toast wafted across Townsville.

Buttercup stopped fighting and sniffed the air. "Something smells good," she said, rubbing her tummy. "I'm actually kind of hungry ..."

"Buttercup, stay focused!" shouted Blossom. "It's trying to distract us!"

"Nice try," said Buttercup, narrowing her

green eyes at the Toaster Monster. "I didn't want toast anyway. I'm in the mood for a sandwich – a **KNUCKLE SANDWICH!**"

SLAM! Buttercup bashed the monster with her fists.

"Yeah, and I want chops!" shouted Bubbles. **"KARATE CHOPS!"**

BLAM! Bubbles aimed karate chops at the monster.

The Toaster Monster's red eyes glared at The Powerpuff Girls. "Get ready to feel the burn!" the monster taunted them. It flicked the knob on its side to **MAXIMUM**. Its insides glowed orange, and smoke billowed out of its top. The horrible smell of burnt toast filled the air.

"Oh no!" cried Blossom. "We've got to stop it before it burns down Townsville!"

The monster lurched through the city centre, crashing through shop windows and knocking down signs. It was so hot that its metal glowed bright red.

WHOOSH! Blossom blasted the Toaster Monster with her ice breath. Cold, sparkling crystals covered the monster, trapping it in ice.

"Way to go, Bloss!" cheered Buttercup.

The monster just laughed and pressed a button marked with a snowflake on its side. "Guess you forgot I had a defrost button," it sneered. Ice melted off the Toaster Monster and it was back in action. Roaring angrily, it used its power cord to lasso a bus and flung it at The Powerpuff Girls.

"We need a plan," said Blossom, as the girls huddled behind a wall. "I say we lead it out of the centre and use the Omega Formation."

"Um … what one's that again?" asked Bubbles.

"Back the monster into a corner then surround him so he can't escape," Blossom explained.

"Oh, yeah," said Bubbles. "I always get that one mixed up with Theta Formation."

Blossom sighed. "I don't know why I bother giving these plans names if nobody can ever remember them."

"Plans are for wusses – I just plan to WIN," Buttercup told her sisters. She zoomed up in the air and hovered in front of the Toaster Monster. "Hey, big guy!" she called. "You think you're so hot, but I hear you can't even handle a bagel."

"How dare you!" the monster bellowed.
"I can turn ANYTHING a crisp golden
brown – even a Powerpuff Girl!" The
metallic monster thundered down the
street, chasing after Blossom.

"YOU ARE GETTING CRUMBS EVERYWHERE!" Blossom
shouted. If there was one thing she hated, it
was mess!

Pink light glowed out of Blossom and
took the shape of a vacuum cleaner.
VROOM! Her vacuum cleaner aura revved
its motor and chased after the Toaster
Monster, gobbling up its trail of crumbs.

With Buttercup leading the way, The
Powerpuff Girls led the Toaster Monster out
of the city centre.

"Down here!" cried Bubbles, pointing to
an alleyway.

The girls forced the monster to the end of the alley. Its red eyes darted around, looking for an escape route, but there was no way out.

"You're in a JAM now!" said Buttercup.

"You'd BUTTER believe it!" said Bubbles.

"Nice one, Bubbs," laughed Buttercup, giving her a high-five.

The Toaster Monster surged forwards, trying to flee, but Bubbles was too fast for it. She grabbed its plug and swung the cord over her head. "Buttercup, catch!" she yelled, throwing the plug through the air. Buttercup zoomed down and grabbed the plug, stretching the cord out in front of the monster's feet. "Now!" Buttercup yelled.

"Here, monster, monster, monster," Blossom called, luring the monster over the tripwire. "Can't catch me! You're just a useless appliance which is going to end up on the scrapheap."

"Is that the best you can do?" Buttercup groaned. But it worked. The toaster monster stepped towards Blossom, and tripped.

"Noooo!" it shrieked as it fell.

Read

HOME SUPER HOME

to find out what happens next!

WHICH POWERPUFF GIRL ARE YOU?

Blossom, Bubbles and Buttercup all LOVE fighting crime, but apart from that our superhero sisters are very different. Which one are you? Take our quiz to find out!

1

Pick a hobby:
A. deathball
B. designing computer games
C. playing board games

2

It's your birthday! What present would you rather get:
A. new roller skates
B. a bunny
C. a stationery set

3

What's your biggest fear?
A. being a wimpybutt
B. not looking cute
C. getting a bad grade at school

4

Which flavour ice cream is the best?
A. pizza
B. bubblegum
C. vanilla with sprinkles

5

Which power would you most like to have:
A. heat vision
B. the ability to talk to animals
C. ice breath

6

Which aura do you think is the most useful?

A. a cannon
B. a dolphin
C. a stapler

7

Your favourite colour is:

A. green
B. blue
C. pink

8

What is you most treasured possession?

A. your musical instrument
B. your soft toy
C. your books

9

When you grow up you want to be:

A. a stuntman
B. a vet
C. the Prime Minister

10

It's Saturday! Would you rather:

A. play sports
B. go on a trip to the zoo
C. do all your homework and tidy your bedroom

NOW COUNT UP YOUR ANSWERS AND FIND OUT WHICH ONE OF THE POWERPUFF GIRLS YOU ARE!

MOSTLY AS

Dude, you are most like Buttercup! You're as cool as a cucumber and you totally rock.

MOSTLY BS

Yippee!!! You are most like Bubbles ... you love animals and you're a real cutie!

MOSTLY CS

We've analysed the data and you made some very smart choices. You are most like Blossom!

FOLLOW THE LINE

Mojo Jojo is planning to cause havoc in Townsville AGAIN!
Can you help Bubbles find the right path to stop him
and save the day?

WORD SEARCH

The Powerpuff Girls need you! There are six things from this book hidden in the wordsearch. Find them all to save Townsville!

- ♥ BLOSSOM
- ♥ BUBBLES
- ♥ MOJO JOJO
- ♥ ICE CREAM
- ♥ PIZZA
- ♥ PLANE

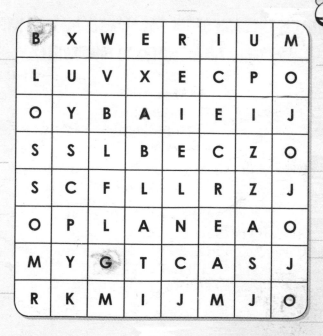

B	X	W	E	R	I	U	M
L	U	V	X	E	C	P	O
O	Y	B	A	I	E	I	J
S	S	L	B	E	C	Z	O
S	C	F	L	L	R	Z	J
O	P	L	A	N	E	A	O
M	Y	G	T	C	A	S	J
R	K	M	I	J	M	J	O

CALLING ALL

the POWERPUFF GIRLS

FANS

We have a POWERPUFF GIRLS toy bundle to give away!
If you want to be in with a chance to receive this
kick-ass prize just answer this question:

WHAT IS THE NAME OF THE EVIL MONKEY MASTERMIND WHO TAKES THE MONSTERS TO TOWNSVILLE?

A) Mojo Yolo
B) Mojo Jojo
C) Hoho Popo

Write your answer on the back of a postcard
and send it to:

Powerpuff Girls Competition
Hachette Children's Group
Carmelite House, 50 Victoria Embankment
London, EC4Y 0DZ
Closing Date: December 2nd 2017

For full terms and conditions go to www.hachettechildrens.co.uk/terms